I0542874

WORKING STIFFS

by

Trinity Marlow

Working Stiffs
ISBN 978-1-937477-75-2
Working Stiffs Copyright © 2012 Trinity Marlow
All rights reserved.

Edited by Carol R. Ward
Cover art by Heidi Sutherlin

These stories are works of fiction and any resemblance to persons, living or dead, or places, events or locales is purely coincidental. The characters are productions of the author's imagination, and used fictitiously.

Table of Contents

THE ENTERTAINER

The Entertainer

Chapter One

Heat rose in Brynn's cheeks as she caught a glimpse of smooth, sculpted male torso peeking out from behind red velvet and white faux fur. Slim hips undulated around the stage to a primal beat while twenty women frantically waved dollar bills at the entertainment for her best friend April's bachelor party. Sexy Santa wasn't like any Santa Brynn had ever seen, and as he shrugged the big coat off his shoulders to reveal the well-muscled chest beneath, she looked away, embarrassed. Her late mother's voice flitted through her head even as she snuck another peek.

Nice girls don't ogle men, dear. And gentlemen don't take their clothes off for money.

The Entertainer

Santa obviously wasn't a gentleman. He was playing with his green suspenders now, pulling them out and slipping them on and off his sculpted shoulders. He must work out every day, she thought, taking another tiny sip of the margarita one of the girls had bought her. Mother wouldn't approve of her drinking, but she always felt a delicious thrill when she did something Mother wouldn't like. Of course it was always followed by a healthy dose of guilt.

She stared, mesmerized as he unclasped the suspenders and swung them over his head, tossing them into the crowd. The volume rose as the girls all scrambled to catch them, and Brynn wondered if they'd be as excited to catch April's bouquet.

A sudden hush made her frown, looking back up to the stage. He wasn't there - where had he gone? She started to rise, pulling her cell phone out of her purse. She hadn't paid good money for Sexy Santa to just disappear before the show was over.

Then the crowd parted and there he was, making his way toward her with a grin on his half-hidden lips. She couldn't really distinguish any of his features, obscured behind a fluffy white beard. A jaunty red and white cap hid all but a few wisps of his dark brown hair. His eyes were emerald and her gaze locked with his as he danced into her personal space. Too close.

The Entertainer

She took a step back, but he followed. There was something about the way he held himself, the confidence in every movement that shook Brynn to her core. The back of her knees hit the chair and she wobbled, gratefully taking his hand to regain her balance. But he pulled her forward instead of letting her go. She resisted, her face flaming with embarrassment as everyone stared. She shook her head, pulling out of his grasp even as she fought the desire to go with him.

Disappointment flashed briefly in his eyes before he turned back to the crowd. April was pushed forward and he ground his hips close to hers before leading her up onto the stage. Brynn drifted back further into the darkness, leaning up against the far wall. She watched him snap off those pants in a quick motion leaving only an upside-down Santa's hat covering his Christmas package. He gyrated over April's lap as she sat in a chair, his tight buns shimmying and the white pom-pom at the tip of his hat shaking wildly.

Brynn shifted, uncomfortably warm as she watched April shake her shoulders and laugh. Friends since grade school, they'd been through everything together from first kisses to the prom and college to careers. April had always been the wild one, grabbing life with both hands even when it didn't work out the way she wanted it to. Brynn had always been the quiet, serious type, and had bailed April out on more than one occasion. When April announced her engagement, Brynn had agreed to be the maid of honor and vowed to throw her friend the best bachelorette party ever.

Calling and making arrangements for a stripper to work the week before Christmas had been difficult, to say the least, but she'd been proud of herself for getting it done. Now as she watched Santa grinding on the bride's lap, she shook her head. She'd always been just the tiniest bit jealous of her friend's ease with men, and couldn't help but wonder what it would be like to have all that male attention focused solely on her.

The music faded away, signaling the end of the last set. Groans filled the room as Santa picked up his clothes and disappeared behind the curtain at the back of the stage. The room felt strangely empty without him, and she briefly considered offering him more money to stay. He didn't come cheap though, and after noting that it was well past midnight already, she decided against it. It was time to start getting people home. She stepped outside the large room and flipped open her phone to key in the limo driver's number. Just as the call connected, a tall, well-built man in tight jeans and a leather jacket approached, familiar emerald eyes sparkling.

"Um, this is Brynn. We're ready to go," she stammered into the phone. At the driver's acknowledgment she hung up, and pretending not to see the stripper, she turned back to the main door. In a swift, obvious move, he stepped wide to block her path, a wide grin on his lips.

"Why are you afraid of me?" he asked, his voice low and smooth. The timbre made her melt inside, even as she felt her face flame red with embarrassment. He moved closer, forcing her to back away until she felt the wall at her shoulders. He braced an arm above her, eyes twinkling with mischief as he waited.

She tried to collect her thoughts, but they refused to cooperate. "I'm not...um...I mean..." He was so close, the heat from his body searing through her clothes and scrambling what was left of her brain. All she could focus on was how those lips would feel if he trailed them down her neck.

The door opened behind him and Brynn knew she was going to die of embarrassment when the women came out in a group, April spotting her immediately. The wicked grin on her best friend's face told her two things - that April was past drunk, and that this was officially going to be the worst night of her life.

"Wow Brynn, if I'd known you had a thing for strippers I'd have bought one for you a long time ago." The crowd laughed, some of the women waving bills in the air.

Brynn cringed. It was one thing to give her a hard time, but to talk about this man like a commodity? "I'm sorry about that," she said quietly, avoiding his eyes. "When she's drunk..."

He hooked a finger under her chin, raising her face a fraction so he could look into her eyes. "It's okay. Comes with the job." He smiled. "It got you talking to me too, so it was worth it."

April bumped her shoulder against his, jostling them both before holding out a pile crumpled cash. "How much for one kiss?" she asked loudly, as wolf whistles and jeers continued behind her.

"This one's on the house," he said, turning to Brynn with a wink. Then his lips were on hers, soft and moist, his tongue tracing the seam of her mouth. She tentatively pressed back, though she didn't have a clue what she was doing, and when he pulled away she dropped her gaze to the floor, mortified. He traced her jaw with two fingers and bent close to her ear. "So sweet," he whispered, dragging his fingers

6

down her neck. "Let me take you home - no strings attached. You don't belong with this group."

She glanced over his shoulder and knew if she stayed she'd never hear the end of it. They had a limo, so no one was driving, and she really didn't want to fend off all the raunchy comments and innuendos that were sure to follow if he just left.

"Okay," she said, before she could change her mind. "Get me out of here."

He straightened, shooting her a devastating grin before grabbing her hand in his and turning to April. "I'm kidnapping your friend," he said, loudly enough that the whole room heard. Brynn was surprised when April frowned, shaking her head.

"I don't think sho," she slurred, swaying on her heels. "You don't know him, Brynn. He could be a murderer or something."

Brynn shook her head. "It's okay. I did a full back-ground check before I hired him. He's fine. Besides, he's just going to..." His grip on her hand increased and she fell silent, wondering what she'd said.

"I promise you'll get her back safe and sound tomorrow morning," he said, tugging her toward the door. "Tonight, she's all mine."

* * *

The Entertainer

Brynn glanced at her rescuer as he drove the classic black Camero out of the parking lot. Sam Ellis was his name, she remembered from the contract she'd had him sign. She hadn't been able to watch the auditions herself, so she'd had the other two bridesmaids choose and then she'd paid for a background check before finalizing the deal by phone. Tonight was the first time she'd seen him and her lips curved up in a little grin. He'd been a good choice, in more ways than one.

"You're thinking too hard."

Brynn jumped at his teasing comment, feeling the heat rise in her cheeks again. "I...um...thank you," she said, shivering as his fingers settled on her thigh.

He chuckled, the smooth sound making her feel things in places she probably shouldn't. "For what?"

"For getting me out of there. And...well, that's it." She looked out the window, licking her lips. Had she really almost thanked him for kissing her? Maybe he hadn't noticed.

"And what?" He stroked her leg, moving his hand briefly to shift into another gear, then putting it back, higher this time. "Come on...don't be shy..."

Damn. She licked her lips again. Maybe...no. She couldn't ask him. He'd never believe her anyway - no one ever did. But he seemed to like her. Maybe if he didn't know...

She turned to face him, grateful for the darkness though she kept her gaze lowered. "And for kissing me. It's...uh, been a long time."

"It was my pleasure, really," he said. She looked up to find him still watching the road, a big grin on his face. "I'd be happy to repeat that particular favor if you want." He pulled into a driveway and turned off the ignition. "Are you going to ask me in?"

Disoriented, she frowned, staring out the windshield at her little house. "How did you know where I live?" Suddenly wary, she reached for the door handle. He put both hands up, laughing.

"Hey, don't freak out. Your friend slipped me your address just before we left. Said something about how you'd better be home when she called later. So here we are. I can leave if you want, no problem." He lowered his hands, reaching for the ignition key.

Brynn reminded herself to breathe. "No, please. I'm sorry." She reached over to place a hand on his arm, the simple touch sending her pulse racing again. "I--I'd like it if you stayed a while."

He removed the keys and stowed them in a pocket, flashing her that sexy smile again. She smiled back and got out of the car, digging in her purse for her keys as he came around the car to join her. He must have noticed her hands were shaking because he reached out to take the keys from her. "Relax," he said, circling her waist with his other arm and propelling her toward the front door. "We aren't going to do anything you don't want to. You're in control tonight."

She wobbled a little on her heels, leaning into his heat as he helped her up the stairs and unlocked her door. They went inside and she flipped the light switch on, illuminating the living room in soft lamplight. This was never going to work. She couldn't possibly seduce a man whose business was seduction. Maybe the direct approach would be best. If he said no, he could just leave and at least it would be quick. She took a deep breath, letting it out slowly as she turned to face him.

"What if I want you to be in control?"

Chapter Two

"I'm not really that kind of guy," Sam said, taking one step back and putting his hands in his the pockets of his jeans. "I mean, I'll tie you up if you want, but I'm not--"

"Oh - no!" Brynn held a hand out, her face burning. "I didn't mean...I don't want...oh hell. This was a bad idea..." She turned away, mortified. This was exactly why she was in her current situation, her inability to ask for what she wanted. She'd finally found the courage only to botch the job and now the hottest-looking prospect in months would turn and walk out the door. Once again she'd be left with a bottle of wine and her vibrator to salvage what was left of the night.

Gentle hands curled over her shoulders, kneading the tension away. "It's okay," Sam said, pulling her back to his chest and crossing his arms around her. "Why don't we start over. What is it you want me to do, exactly? Don't be shy." He stroked long fingers down the side of her neck, the motion soothing.

She relaxed into his embrace and sighed. It was now or never. "I want you to teach me about sex," she blurted, thankful she didn't have to face him. His grip loosened slightly.

"Are you a virgin?" The tone of his question as he breathed it in her ear warned her that any answer other than 'no' would be unacceptable. But she already knew that. The last guy she'd told had nearly tripped over her coffee table on his way out the door.

She shook her head. "No, of course not. I just don't have much experience and I want...well, I just don't know what makes it...good, I guess."

Sam chuckled in her ear, his arms tightening around her again. "If sex is just 'good', you're doing it wrong, sweetheart." His right hand moved lower to skim her left breast, his middle finger circling her pebbled nipple as his lips nibbled at the spot where her shoulder and neck met. She shivered, her head falling back on his shoulder as he moved his other hand to play with her other breast. She wasn't sure what to do with her arms - they seemed to be in the way.

Apparently sensing her quandary, Sam grasped her wrists, raising them behind her head to his neck and then lowering his own to her rib cage. Instinctively she ran her fingers through his hair, caressed his neck as he kissed his way across the top of her shoulder. His fingers found their way under the hem of her shirt to play against her bare skin sending warm impulses through her body and down between her legs. A whimper escaped her lips and she clamped them shut, tensing as he slipped one hand into the waistband of her jeans.

"What's wrong?" he murmured, withdrawing and putting his hands on her hips. "If you're uncomfortable with this..." He held her away and for a moment she thought he might leave. Brynn turned to face him, relieved at the kind smile on his lips.

"Nothing's wrong," she said, forcing herself to look into his eyes. "I just don't really know what to do." She gave a nervous laugh. "This is so stupid. I'm sorry. I--"

"You're thinking too much." Sam took her hand and pulled her forward. "Let's try something different." He cupped the side of her face with his palm and before she could move he leaned in to cover her lips with his own.

* * *

Whoa. Brynn couldn't hold back another soft whimper. His lips were so soft, so...demanding. Her eyes fluttered closed, her hands moving up around his neck of their own accord. His tongue pushed past her lips, plundering her mouth and she met it with her own, instinct taking over. She'd been kissed before, even with tongue, but none had ever been like this. Warmth infused her whole body and when he pulled back, she leaned toward him, her cheeks heating when she realized what she'd done.

"Open your eyes," Sam said, his voice soft. She forced them open, his gentle smile easing some of her embarrassment. "Better?"

She nodded, afraid to speak lest she break the spell. He ran his fingers over one side of her neck, each stroke sending a shimmer of pleasure through her skin. He leaned down, kissing a spot just under her ear. "Do you think we might be more comfortable in the bedroom?" His hot whisper against her skin sent a rush of liquid heat between her legs and her knees nearly gave out.

14

"Yesss..." she hissed, taking in a sharp breath as two fingers lightly pinched one of her nipples.

Sam chuckled into her ear, rubbing the underside of her breast with his fingers before he stepped back, severing all contact. She reached for him, but he evaded her grasp. She looked up at him, confused at his knowing grin. "Sorry sweetheart, but you're going to have to give me directions, and I suspect you can't do that if I'm touching you."

Her face flamed and she wished she hadn't turned on the light as she pointed to the hall. "Uh...last door on the right. I think I'll just get a quick glass of water..."

He chuckled, grabbing her hand. "Oh no you don't. Don't go thinking again." He pulled her in for a quick kiss, then led her down the hall to her room. She expected him to turn on the lights but he didn't. Instead he simply shut the door, put his hands on her hips and pressed kisses down the side of her neck.

"Oh god," she breathed, tilting her head to allow him better access. "That feels so good."

He pushed her shirt up over her breasts, leaned back and pulled it off over her head. The darkness provided her courage and as he licked and suckled his way down her chest, she found the hem of his shirt and skimmed it up his body, her fingers exploring his rib cage along the way. He leaned back long enough to pull it over his head and then planted a long, searing kiss on her mouth as he walked her backwards to the bed. Her knees hit the edge and she didn't resist, falling horizontal as he came down over her.

Running her fingers through his hair she arched up as he laved at a hard nipple. The action sent electrical impulses straight down to her core, and she squirmed, her clit begging for attention. As if he could read her mind, he reached between them and pressed a finger against her heat, fanning the flames higher.

"More. Please." She wiggled against him, frustrated by the barrier of her jeans and panties. Then the pressure was gone, and she nearly cried out in frustration.

He kissed her lips, smiling against them as his fingers worked at the button of her pants. "Shh...it's okay. Patience, sweetheart." Leaving a trail of kisses down the center of her body, he moved lower until he could shimmy the offending clothes off her hips and onto the floor. Fabric rustled and Brynn let her legs fall open as she waited for him to return. Not disappointed for long, soon she felt his fingers tickling up between her legs, pushing them apart as he stepped between them. A finger traced her inner lips, smoothing over and around lubricating her with her own cream. Then she felt his breath on her core and time all but stopped as his tongue licked her most sensitive nub and sent her nerves soaring.

She reached down to run her fingers through the thick curls on his head as he pushed one finger inside her. She moaned low as he worked in and out, adding a second finger to stretch her passage. His tongue swirled round and round, sending her higher and higher as his fingers pumped in and out, bringing her closer to something she'd never quite been able to grasp.

Then he turned his fingers just so and curled the tips, at the same time he sucked down hard on her clit, and the world exploded into a million different colors as her whole body spiraled out of control.

Chapter Three

Gentle touches and soft murmurs slowly pulled Brynn back to earth. "Wow," she breathed, not daring to open her eyes lest the illusion shatter. Warm breath wafted over her ear as moist kisses kept the nerves in her neck alert.

"That's it," Sam said, his voice soothing, his body cradled between her legs. "Just ride it out, babe."

Babe. The near-endearment reminded her not to mistake lust for love, or to hope that this encounter was anything more than sex. She brought her legs up to circle his hips, her ankles holding him close as his cock moved slowly back and forth over her center. Her skin was still super-charged and every place he touched her cried out for more. His fingertips grazed her nipple, petting the hard nub back and forth, round and round as she arched up, begging for more.

"Sam?" Her voice sounded odd, even to her own ears as she rasped his name.

"Yes Brynn?"

"I want you..."

"Want me how?"

"I...uh..inside me. Now."

He chuckled, leaning down to press his lips to hers. "Open your eyes."

She slid her hands up over his shoulders. "No." She shook her head, knowing she was being unreasonable. "If I open my eyes, I'll think again. And I don't want to think anymore." She felt his kiss against each of her eyes in turn, then his hand smoothing her hair back from her forehead.

"Come on," he coaxed, pausing to suckle the hollow of her throat. "I promise I won't let you think."

Brynn inhaled, focusing on what his hand was doing to her breast as she reluctantly opened her eyes. As soon as she looked up at him, he moved just so and thrust into her core.

She gasped, arching up at the unfamiliar feeling of invasion. He felt good, but big, and she was grateful when he remained still, allowing her body to adjust to his girth.

"God you're tight," he hissed, his muscles tensed as he braced over her. She reminded herself to breath, her fingers tracing the ridges that defined his chest and arms as he pulsed within her. So this was it then. Sex. A rush of liquid heat between her thighs made her thankful for the darkness so he couldn't see her blush.

He kissed her once, then twice, pulling out slightly then pushing back in. Her body had never felt more alive as the tension coiled between her legs. She closed her eyes, tentatively moving her lower body to meet his thrusts, earning a low growl as a fingernail grazed his flat nipple. He urged her on, faster, and her movements became almost frantic as her skin tingled and every bit of her focus zeroed in on the new sensations between her legs. She whimpered, unable to help herself and nearly cried out when his lips closed over her nipple and sucked hard. Then he slid one hand between their bodies and pressed a finger to her clit, triggering an orgasm so hard she nearly came off the bed, arching up and falling back in succession as the waves of completion washed over her.

Sam groaned, then thrust hard and long, once, twice, three times until he was spent. Then he collapsed on top of her, folding her in his arms and rolling them both to the side. She lay in his arms, just breathing until he pulled away, stroking the side of her face with one hand.

"That was incredible," he said, looking into her eyes. Even in the dark she could see he was sincere, and she was grateful. "I'll be right back."

After he left, Brynn pulled the covers back and crawled between the sheets. It had been such a long day and she was so very tired...would he stay? Would he go? She wasn't sure what the proper etiquette was for one-night-stands, but she was fairly sure she'd already broken several. He padded back in and she waited, wondering what could possibly break the now-awkward silence.

Sam slipped into bed, and reached for her, pulling her tight against his side as he lay on his back. She rested her head tentatively on his shoulder, and he hugged her close, kissing her head. "Are you okay?"

Brynn frowned, mentally taking stock. "I think so...is there some reason I shouldn't be?"

He chuckled, squeezing the arm around her shoulders. "Of course not. When was the last time you slept with someone, anyway?" She tensed, her pulse beating faster again. It was now or never. Maybe never was better. But she wanted him to know he was special, and she'd always think fondly of him after to-night.

"Actually," she said, her body trembling against his, "I am--was, that is, a virgin."

* * *

Sam was quiet for a long moment. Brynn wondered if he'd heard her, and raised her head off his chest just as he chuckled, the sound vibrating under her hand on his chest. She frowned, propping herself up on one elbow so she could see his face. "What's so funny?"

He shook his head, the grin on his lips an extra insult. "Honey, you were no virgin. A man can tell - didn't anyone ever tell you that?"

Brynn rolled away from him, pulling the covers up over her naked body and wondering why she'd thought he'd be different. "I know, but it's not like that. I was dating this guy in college, and we played around, but I wasn't ready. One night he tried to show me...um...with his fingers..." She took a breath, focused enough to note that Sam had stopped laughing. A good sign, she hoped. "Anyway, it hurt. A lot, and I made him leave.

"Did I hurt you?"

The Entertainer

Brynn shivered at the cold note in Sam's voice. Why hadn't she kept her mouth shut? "No, of course not." The mattress shifted and she glanced over to see Sam swinging his legs over the edge of the bed. How long would it take him to find his clothes? Clearly this was the part where he ran away. Just like everyone else.

"How does a woman get to be your age without having sex?" He rubbed his face with his hands, his back to her presenting a perfect silhouette from the window. "Why didn't you tell me before? This would never--"

"This would never have happened. I know," Brynn said, anger replacing humiliation in a heartbeat. "How would you know how old I am? You make me sound like an old hag or something." She crossed her arms over her chest, her body humming for an entirely different reason than it had minutes before. "Look, I don't owe you any explanations, and you don't owe me anything either. I wanted to know what sex was like, and you...helped me." She scooted off the bed, reaching for the robe she kept on a chair nearby. Covering herself, she turned to see Sam pulling on his jeans. "I shouldn't have told you. I'm sorry. I'm sure you remember the way out."

She went down the hall to the bathroom and locked the door, blinking back the tears that threatened to fall. It wasn't the one-night stand that bothered her. She'd known from the start this was just about sex, but the fact that she hadn't had the time or inclination to lose her virginity before now just shouldn't be that big of a deal. So what if she was older than the average teenager? At least it wouldn't be an issue from now on. Thank God.

Shaking her head, she started the shower and hung her robe on the back of the door. Screw him, she thought as she stepped under the warm spray. Her body felt strangely light and sensitive under the water and she grinned, realizing she'd done just that. Finally.

Chapter Four

One week later, Brynn's feet were already killing her as she stood at the back of the church. She glanced down at her chest again and wished the bouquet she had to carry was bigger. Tight red taffeta with no room for a padded bra underneath was so not a good idea for a Christmas wedding. She shivered, her only consolation the hope that the wedding guests would focus on the goosebumps on her arms instead of her cleavage. At least she'd be facing the front of the church while April and Luke said their vows.

"Everyone ready?" The wedding planner's sing-song voice grated nearly as bad as the strappy silver stilettos as Brynn took her place in line behind the other bridesmaids beside the best man. She took his arm, all-too-aware of how bad her wardrobe problem was judging from the direction of his stare. He wasn't bad looking, actually - the quintessential tall, dark and handsome. Wire-rimmed glasses accented his angular face nicely, and she tried to imagine his thin lips warming up one of her hardened nipples. The face that looked up at her in her mind wasn't his though.

As the familiar music started, she wondered for the five-thousandth time if she should have called the number Sam had left for her that night. The note had said to call, but she was old enough to know that it probably didn't mean anything, he was just trying to be nice to the poor, clingy virgin who'd tricked him into deflowering her. She'd thrown the number out, afraid that if she kept it she'd break down and call. She had too much pride to play that girl and she'd be damned if she'd impose on him any further.

Still, she thought as her escort led her into the sanctuary, sleeping with him had created a problem. Now that she'd had a taste, she wanted more, but picking out a guy wasn't any easier than it was before. Her vibrator helped, but it just wasn't quite enough anymore. She glanced at the man beside her again who looked down at her...chest. Heck, maybe she should just go for it. He seemed amiable to the idea, at least.

The Entertainer

Smothering a grin, she took her place on the top step of the stage and turned to watch April make her big entrance. A flashbulb reminded her to reposition herself so that only the preacher and the musician had a good view, a fact that nearly made her laugh. She craned her neck, somehow managing to hold the position until the bride and groom were positioned above her on the platform. Grateful that the preacher seemed focused on the happy couple, she snuck a sideways glance at the organist, sure that the old lady would be shooting her dirty looks for her display. To her dismay, it wasn't a little old lady sitting on the bench and she nearly dropped the bride's bouquet she was holding along with her own.

Sam winked at her, sending heat rushing both up to her face and down between her legs. Mortified that her skin probably matched her dress and her thong was uncomfortably damp, she turned to face the preacher. What on earth was a stripper doing playing the organ at a wedding? Was that even allowed by the church? She shifted, trying to relieve the pressure from her left foot and her right heel slipped off the step. Luckily the girl behind her must have seen it and put a stabilizing hand at her back. She looked over her shoulder with an apologetic smile and spent the rest of the ceremony with both feet locked firmly in place, her eyes glued to the preacher. It seemed like the safest strategy all around at that point.

When it was finally over, Brynn slipped out of the receiving line, knowing April would be angry but past the point of caring. She hobbled down a back hall until she found a restroom and slipped inside, grateful to see an old fashioned couch just inside the door. She sat down, immediately kicking her shoes off with a sigh, just as the door opened again.

"I thought I might see you today," Sam said, grinning as he walked toward her, a roll of silver duct tape in his hand.

* * *

"What are you doing here? And...uh, what's that for?" Brynn eyed the duct tape in Sam's hand as he moved closer. Please don't be a serial killer...

"I'm a man of many talents," he said kneeling down in front of her and lifting one of her feet in his hands. "You seemed uncomfortable during the ceremony, and as much as I love seeing those pretty nipples poking at your dress, the tape will keep everyone from staring for the rest of the evening." His fingers were kneading her foot with magical circular strokes, pain fading into blissful relaxation.

The Entertainer

"Oh God, that feels so good..." she closed her eyes and leaned back, completely focused on the soothing warmth radiating up first one leg, then the other as he switched feet. "You are so hired," she moaned, trying to forget that she still had to get through the reception. That luxurious touch moved up her leg, caressing her calf and rounding her knee before sliding ever so slowly up each thigh. Her breathing quickened as she felt her dress being pushed up, her legs parted, and hot, long breaths against her center. He lapped at her lace panties, adding to the moist heat already there. She whimpered, spreading her legs wider as he pushed the scrap of fabric aside and entered her with one finger, then two, then three. As he thrust in and out, awakening her most sensitive spots once again she writhed half-on, half-off the sofa, imagining how wanton she must look lying there with her dress bunched around her waist and Sam's head between her legs. Just then his tongue flicked her clit, keeping time with one, two, three deep thrusts. It was too much, and her whole body stiffened as sweet, mind-numbing sensations took away all control.

She slid off the couch onto Sam's lap, his fingers still inside her, his thumb gently circling her sensitive nub. His mouth closed hard over hers, wild, possessive, and she arched against his chest as he held her tight, working her core as he whispered softly into her ear.

"Come again. Now."

Her fingers locked onto his shoulders as the intense, blinding pleasure washed over her once more. She held on tight, her muscles spasming around him as he stroked slow and smooth within her. When she could finally breathe, he pulled back just enough to bring his wet fingers to his mouth. His eyes locked on hers as he sucked each one clean, then kissed her long and slow. She tasted herself on his tongue, musky and sweet. His hands moved up her back, grasping the zipper of her dress and pulling it down slowly. Stopping half-way, he leaned back and slid the dress and her thin strapless tube bra down to expose her breasts. She shivered, not at the loss of the thin barrier, but at the hunger in his eyes.

"You have beautiful tits," he murmured, bending to suck one hard nub between his lips. He grazed the peak with his teeth, pulling it out just to the point of pain before releasing it. Brynn panted, arching up and offering her other breast to him as she supported her head on the couch, her eyes closed in bliss as he suckled and nipped at her other breast.

The Entertainer

A ripping sound brought her partially out of the fog. Had the dress succumbed to the rough handling? Then she felt something cold pressed against her skin and finally opened her eyes, looking down to find two strips of duct tape centered over each nipple in the shape of a cross.

Chapter Five

"You want me to wear tape over my...um, here?" Brynn sat up, her fingers instinctively reaching up to smooth over the silver strips. "I guess that's one way to fix it."

Sam chuckled. "It's all I could come up with at the moment, but I can't say I'm sorry. It's a very sexy look for you."

"Uh, yeah. I really appreciate you fixing my problem, but you don't have to lie to make me feel better. I should head downstairs. April's probably beside herself by now, with as much time as I've been gone. I'm a horrible maid of honor." She started to pull up the tiny bra, but Sam's hand halted her movements.

"Not so fast," he said, getting to his feet. He helped her up, then twirled her around to face a full-length mirror on the opposite wall. Standing behind her, he supported one breast in each hand, watching over her shoulder. "Look at that. Sometimes what you can't see is just as provocative as what you can, wouldn't you say?"

She nodded, her body too warm as she looked at herself on display. A wanton vixen stared back, clearly at the mercy of her man. She imagined what she'd look like with another piece of duct tape around her neck, like a wide, fitted collar. Her face turned the same shade as her dress at the wicked thought. "I really should go." She pushed out of his embrace and put her bodice back together, struggling with the low zipper in back.

"Here, let me." He brushed her hands away and raised the metal clasp to the middle of her back, his knuckles grazing her bare shoulders. She looked in the mirror once more, giving the front of her dress a good tug north before she turned to go.

"About the other night..."

She stopped and smiled over her shoulder at him. "It's fine, Sam. I didn't expect anything from you then, and I don't expect anything from you now. We were just having a little fun - no need to get all girly about it." She puckered her lips and blew him a kiss before she left, closing the door behind her.

* * *

Just a little fun. Her words haunted her as she made her way to the basement, slipping off her shoes as she reached the reception hall. She wanted it to be true. She didn't want to want him, but damned if she wasn't the same as all the rest of those silly women who fell for the first guy who slept with them. She shook her head, breathing in deep and letting it out slow. Maybe all she had to do was have sex with someone else to break this infatuation with Sam.

She scanned the room, her gaze landing on the best man seated at the head table with the rest of the wedding party. Spotting an empty chair beside him, she moved toward him, stopping briefly to apologize to April for ducking out earlier. Finally she stood in front of him, bending down to give him a good peek as she placed her lips close to his ear. "Is this seat taken?"

"It is now." He lightly trailed a finger along the inner curve of her breast, skimming the center of her cleavage as she sat down. She leaned into his touch, surprised when her body responded. Apparently it was only her head that longed for Sam. Sitting back, she placed a hand on the best man's thigh, disappointed at her own disloyalty. Except there was no reason to be loyal to Sam, was there? Confused, she jumped as a slow melody drifted through the room. The lights dimmed, and she swiveled in her chair to where the floor had been cleared for dancing.

"Good evening, ladies and gentlemen. I'm Sam, and I'll be your DJ tonight. Let's get started with a nice slow dance for the bride and groom. Congratulations to the lovely couple." Applause rippled through the crowd as Luke pulled April into his arms and swung her around, holding her close as they swayed to the music.

Brynn reached for a water glass on the table, gulping down half the liquid before setting it down. Hot. She was hot, and not because the best man was nibbling at her neck from behind. Sam was here too? Suddenly his earlier comment made sense. A man of many talents indeed.

She scanned the area at the back of the room, finally spotting him on a raised platform in the back corner. Unable to see his face, she wondered what he was thinking as he stood there, watching her with another man. The song segued into a slightly faster beat, and she decided she may as well find out. Glancing over her shoulder, she smiled at the best man.

"I'm Brynn," she said, holding out her hand to shake his. "What's your name?"

"Patrick." He took her hand, raising it to his lips and lightly kissing her fingers.

She smiled, charmed by the gesture. "Nice to meet you, Patrick. Would you like to dance?"

He stood, helping her up with a grin. "It's not my first choice, but it'll do for now." His husky voice held a sensual promise, but Brynn was dismayed to find her gaze wandering back to Sam. She had to stop this...obsession now, before she really did turn into one of those clingy women men ran from. Stepping onto the dance floor, she forced herself into the circle of Patrick's arms, smiling up at him like he was the only man on earth. His hips ground against hers as they swayed, his erection brushing her pelvis with every other movement. She felt flushed as she ran her hands over his broad chest, her dress suddenly too confining. She'd left her panties in the bathroom garbage - they'd been too wet to wear after her encounter with Sam, and moisture slicked her thighs as Patrick caressed her ass with one hand and traced a finger over the swell of her breast with the other. All the while, Sam's stare burned into her back, almost as if he were right behind her.

The Entertainer

Then Patrick pulled his lips away from her neck, his eyes fixed on something over her shoulder. She turned in his arms, her butt cradling Patrick's hard cock as she looked into Sam's gorgeous eyes.

Chapter Six

"Having fun, sweetheart?" Sam winked, an amused expression on his face as he stood watching, hands tucked casually in his pockets.

Brynn grabbed Patrick's hands when he started to back away, pulling him tight against her back and pressing his fingers just under her breasts. She nodded, her pulse racing in anticipation of...something. "Best wedding reception ever," she said, her hips still moving slightly to the music. "Are you having fun?"

He gave a slight laugh. "More than you know. Who's your friend?" Confidence rolled off him in waves, and Brynn shook her head. He really wasn't jealous. How did guys do that?"

"This is Patrick," she said, glancing over her shoulder, briefly. "He's the best man."

The Entertainer

Sam held out his hand, his knuckles brushing her breast as he grasped Patrick's. "So it appears," he quipped, not stepping back like she thought he would. "The thing is..." he reached out to touch her neck, one finger running just down the side and over her shoulder. "I wonder if one man will be enough, even at his best."

"I was wondering the same thing," Patrick murmured in her ear, his hot breath sending shivers down her spine. Her knees nearly buckled as Sam took a step forward, brushing a hair from her face.

"Brynn?" April's voice barely broke through the sensual haze the two men had wrapped her in. "Oh my god, Brynn. I need to talk to you. Right. Now."

The fog began to dissipate as she found herself tugged out of Patrick's grasp, out from between the two men who were clearly planning to rock her world. Together. She stumbled up the basement stairs after her best friend, glad she'd ditched the heels until the reached the front door and April pulled her out into the frigid night air.

"What the hell?" she said, the cold air hitting her lungs hard. She yanked her wrist free and turned back, swinging the door open wide as she reentered the church lobby. April followed, breathing hard and staring at Brynn with narrowed eyes.

"Do you have any idea how many people were staring at you? My parents think Patrick must have drugged you! " She paced in front of the stairwell, her hands moving fast as she lectured. "You're always the good one. Of all the people I thought would ruin my reception, the last person I expected was you. What on earth has gotten into you, Brynn?"

Sex. Brynn couldn't stop her lips from turning up at the thought, earning an exasperated gesture from the bride as she took a seat on the steps leading up to the sanctuary. Then it occurred to her that April might have some experience with the position she'd nearly found herself in. "Have you ever slept with two men?"

"You did not seriously just ask me that on my wedding night."

Brynn shrugged. "If any of my friends would know, it would be you." For a moment April seemed to consider answering, and then she shook her head, as if shaking out any stray memories.

"I can't do this. Not tonight. I thought you would understand. I thought maybe just having you here would keep me from...doing the crazy stuff I always do." She looked down at Brynn, her eyes pleading. "What happened to the old Brynn? Why are you being like this?"

"You mean being like you?" Brynn couldn't resist the jab, but immediately wished she could take it back. "I'm sorry, I just...I never knew sex would make me have all these feelings and urges--"

"Whoa." April flopped down on the step beside her, folding what she could of her train in her lap. "Back up there. What do you mean, you never knew? You can't tell me you were a vir--"

"Yes, I was a virgin until a week ago. No one ever believes me, but now you know." Brynn looked down at her hands, the familiar unease creeping into her brain. "Even Sam didn't believe me, and who could blame him? It was stupid to put it off so long." She stood, wandering to the door and peering out into the night. "I guess I did sort of go a little crazy, huh? But Sam is so...and Patrick..." She turned to look at April, who was nodding her head. "You do know what I mean then."

The bride sighed. "I do. I just wish you wouldn't have picked my reception to explore your new needs."

Footsteps on the stairs caught Brynn's attention, and she wasn't sure if she was relieved or not to see Patrick ascending, Sam following close behind.

"We wanted to apologize," Patrick said as the two men stood in front of Brynn and April. Brynn's cheeks heated, the urge to run and hide from both of them strong. "We're sorry for any trouble we caused. Will you forgive us?"

April shrugged, getting up from the stairs. "It's okay, I guess. Brynn explained and while I'm still not happy, I suppose there's no real harm done. Just...no more, okay? I think it would be best if you all left." She winked at Brynn. "I suspect that's what you want to do anyway, right?"

Brynn stood, her body on fire at the smug grins worn by Sam and Patrick. Had she really been considering sleeping with both of them? How had it all gotten so out of hand? "Actually, you're right. I've had enough fun for one night. I think I'll head home." She glanced at the men, who turned to follow her as she walked past them toward the basement steps to retrieve her shoes and coat. "Alone."

* * *

Half an hour later, Brynn unlocked her door and hung her purse on its hook. She slid her feet into her slippers and padded back toward the bedroom. A hot bath and her vibrator might help take the remaining edge off the night. She unzipped her dress, letting it fall to the floor, then removed the plain tube bra, her fingers skimming the duct tape Sam had covered her nipples with. Walking to the mirror, she cupped a breast in each hand, the sight of those gray crosses sending more moisture slicking between her naked thighs. Her head tilted, regarding the curly bush that covered her mound. Maybe she should shave it? She lowered one hand, her fingers moving gently over her clit as she watched, imagining what it would look like hairless. Maybe she'd try that next. Her eyes went back up as she continued to finger herself.

The doorbell rang. Brynn jumped, her pulse racing as her hands fell to her sides. Who could it be at this hour? Maybe she just wouldn't answer...

Two knocks were followed by another ring, and she sighed, reaching for her fuzzy bathrobe. Belting it tightly at her waist, she went to the door and checked the peephole. Sam stood on the other side, his expression serious. She opened the door.

"What's wrong?" she asked, standing back to let him enter. He waited until she closed and locked the door before walking down the hall to the living room. She followed, frowning as he took a seat on her sofa, patting the spot beside him. She sat sideways, adjusting her robe to cover her leg and leaned forward. "Sam, what is it? What's wrong?"

He shook his head, bracing one arm beside her on the back of the couch. "It's not really wrong, I just...I think I made a mistake. And I'm hoping you can help me fix it." He looked into her eyes, his gaze intense. "I need you to be honest with me. Why did you come on to the best man?" Brynn frowned, opening her mouth, but he put three fingers against her lips to stop her. "Was it because I wasn't enough for you? Because you wanted to explore? Or were you maybe, possibly trying to make me jealous?"

She shook her head and stood to walk away, but a strong arm caught her around the waist and pulled her backwards. She fell onto Sam's lap, his erection pressing into her butt as he held her in place with both arms. "What are you doing? Let me go!" She struggled, but they both knew it was just a token. When she stilled, Sam leaned down, placing a gentle, chaste kiss on her lips.

"I think you wanted to make me jealous." She shook her head again, but he just smiled. "You were trying to see what I'd do seeing you with another man, and it kind of got out of control, didn't it?"

She thought about arguing, but he was so close to the truth, she simply lowered her eyes to his chest, absently playing with one of his shirt buttons. Maybe if she told him, he could help her figure things out. "I...I kept thinking about you, but I didn't want to be clingy. I didn't want to be that girl. So I thought maybe if I slept with someone else...and then you were there..." she stopped, not sure what else to say. It sounded so stupid. She should have kept her mouth shut.

"Brynn. Look at me."

She lifted her head, slowly. He smiled, a reassuring gesture that sent tingles down the back of her neck. "I guess that's pretty stupid, huh? Like I'm some silly high-school kid, instead of a grown woman."

"I've been thinking about you too, you know." The words wrapped around her like soft velvet, soothing her fears. "I'm sorry I made you feel like I didn't want to see you again because you--because I was your first. I do, very much want to see you again." He traced a finger from her neck down the inside of her collar, his touch fire against her skin.

"Really?" She cringed, looking down as soon as the word was out. Could she sound any more needy?

He chuckled, that deep voice vibrating through her body and down between her legs. "Really. I mean, if you want to experiment with two guys sometime, that's okay too, but I'd like to explore just us for now, if that's okay with you."

She half-laughed, half-sobbed, leaning into his chest and pressing her face against his neck. "I'd really like that," she said, her hand caressing his chest through his shirt. "Thank you," she whispered, pressing a soft kiss to his jaw. One of his hands slipped inside her robe, cupping a breast. He laughed, his fingers tracing the tape he'd put on earlier.

"I think we can probably take these off now, don't you think?"

Brynn nodded, pulling back to look in to those bright, sexy green eyes. "I was just waiting for you."

###

THE
PILE DRIVER

The Pile Driver

48

Chapter One

Dawn's fingers flew over the keyboard as she made a point of ignoring the two skinny redheads looking out the window. It wasn't much of a view, considering the crew had just started the foundation work, but the girls weren't looking at the piles of dirt and big machines anyway. Where on earth had Eric managed to find real, honest-to-goodness bimbo twins? She really wanted to know, so she could avoid the place like the plague.

"What do you think a pile driver really does, anyway?" Redhead number one snapped her gum so loud Dawn nearly knocked over her water glass.

Redhead number two grinned. "You'd know if you hadn't fallen asleep so early last night, silly." Both girls dissolved into giggles, their tight leopard-print

dresses practically begging for a little breathing room.
Holding on to each other to avoid falling off their
matching wedge sandals, the girls drew appreciative
smiles from the builder and the architect who were
discussing changes over coffee at the conference
table.

"A pile driver operates heavy equipment to help
put in the foundations for buildings and other struc-
tures," Dawn said, staring down the giggling women.
"The name is actually the name of a group of machines designed to drive pilings - those big round ce-
ment fixtures - into the ground." The twins looked at
each other for a moment, and burst out laughing just
as the trailer door swung open.

Eric stepped inside, his white tee no longer white
and a fine layer of black grime covering most of his
exposed skin. Even so, Dawn had to admit that it was
part of his appeal, and it was all she could do to keep
from sneering as his fan club of the day ran up and
tackled him, one on each side. Not that he couldn't
handle it. Six foot two and all muscle, the man had
the body of a professional wrestler. Dawn had been
fantasizing about it since she started working for the
construction company three years ago.

Not that he would notice. Dawn turned back to
her computer screen and pretended to be working.

The man was a chick magnet - a new woman on his arm nearly every night. But not just any girls - he always seemed to come back with the good looking, fake boobs and impossible heels sort. Never just your average woman...and certainly not one who still wore flannel shirts long after the trend was over.

From the corner of her eye, Dawn saw him pick up both twins at once and swing them around in a circle. She shook her head, tapping away at her spreadsheet even though she knew full well she'd have to redo it when the office quieted down.

"We're headed to Elmo's for dinner," Eric said, putting the girls on their feet. At least they looked like they were of age this time. "Anyone wanna come? Dawn?"

She shook her head and waved him off, a pencil between her teeth.

"Suit yourself," he said, and shortly afterward she let out the breath she'd been holding as the door banged shut behind the trio.

The architect left too and Harry Stanton, the builder, approached her desk. "You know everyone knows you have a thing for that man," he said, smiling kindly. She shook her head, putting the well-chewed pencil in a cup, smiling in spite of herself.

Harry was like a father to her, though sometimes he took his role a little too seriously.

"Now don't go spreading lies, Harry," she said, giving him a stern look. "There's no way I'd date a construction worker. Eric Daniels is off limits, and it's just as well, given how he seems to go through women like tissues. I think those two were the sixth and seventh just this month."

Harry winked. "Not that you're counting, right?" He shook his head. "I think you'd be surprised if you got to know him. He's smart under all that brawn. Give the man a chance."

"Give what man a chance?" Eric walked back in and picked up his wallet from the table, holding it up by way of explanation. "Forgot this. Are you having man troubles, Dawn?"

"No, I am not," Dawn said, thankful the lighting was dim, given how warm her cheeks were. She shot Harry a warning look. "You stay out of my love life." Then she forced herself to look Eric in the eyes. "And you mind your own business. Don't you have...two girls waiting for you?" She barely managed to refrain from calling them bimbos, but judging from the way he was looking at her, as if he could read her thoughts, he already knew her feelings on the subject.

"Girls, yes." He leaned against the doorway; his expression taking on a quality Dawn didn't quite know what to do with. The intensity made her want to squirm in her seat - in a good way - as he continued. "A woman, no. So if you wanna take their place, say the word and they're gone."

Dawn shook her head. "Um, no thanks. You go have fun with your little friends. I still have some work to finish up here. Now skedaddle, both of you." She swiveled her chair back around to face her computer screen, hoping they'd both just leave.

"Don't mind her, son," Harry said, his boots thudding lightly across the floor behind her. "She's tired, and between you and me..."

Dawn couldn't hear the rest, and she turned around to give both men a dirty look just as the door swung shut behind them. Relieved, she sat back in her chair and let out a long breath. For just a moment she let herself wonder what it would have been like to say yes. The way he'd looked at her...it surprised her that he'd managed to distinguish between her and his toys for the evening. Though maybe that's how he did it with all the girls - treated them like they were special to their face, and then talked down about them behind their backs. Maybe he was telling the twins all about how the office manager was just a nobody.

53

Nah. She shook her head and turned back to the screen. Those girls weren't threatened by someone like Dawn. They didn't need to be, with their perfect bodies and hair down to there. They knew they could hold a man's attention. "And they're welcome to him," Dawn murmured, opening up the spreadsheet she'd been trying to balance earlier when Eric's fan club had interrupted.

When her cell phone rang, Dawn jumped at the intrusive sound. Glancing at the clock as she got it off the desk, she was shocked that nearly two hours had passed. She was almost done balancing the budget for this particular project though, which had been her goal for the day.

"Hello?" she said, noting her best friend Amy's number on the caller ID. Probably calling to see if she wanted to go out for drinks, and Dawn was definitely ready for a margarita.

"Dawn, you have to come get me. Please. I had a double date with this guy, and Sam turned out to be the other guy, and they just got into this huge fight and the other girl--"

"Whoa," Dawn said, reaching over to shut down her computer. "Slow down, and tell me where you are first. I can leave now..." She got her purse from the desk drawer and slung it over her shoulder.

Amy sniffled into her ear. "I'm at Elmo's, but in the alley. I don't know where Sam went, and my date, Jeremy, just left me here when he found out that Sam and I...oh god, Dawn, you have to hurry. You know what Sam did last time, and Sergeant Bransen isn't picking up!"

Dawn opened the car door and belted herself in, then started the engine. "I'm coming right now - I have to hang up so I can drive, but you need to do something for me. Are you listening? This is important."

"I'm listening," Amy sniffled again.

"Good," Dawn could only think of one thing that would keep Amy safe until she got there. "Go inside, and find a guy with a couple of redheaded twins hanging on him. His name is Eric. Tell him Dawn said you should stay with him until I get there. Don't leave his side until you see me, okay? He can handle Sam. We'll figure out how to get a hold of Bransen after I get you out of there."

"What's your friend's name again?" Amy said, the background noise getting louder in Dawn's ear. "Oh wait, there's a guy with twins. Wow, he's really cute. I'll just... No! Sam, let me go..."

Chapter Two

Taking the corner way too fast, Dawn pulled up to an empty spot half a block away from Elmo's and cut the engine. The bar and grill was a favorite of the local factory and construction workers, and cars lined both sides of the street while loud music pumped out through open doors. Two police cars with lights flashing were parked in the middle of the parking lot, and her heart raced as she ran to the door and slipped inside, craning her head as she scanned the room for Eric's tall profile. Please let her be okay, she thought, biting her lower lip as she started walking toward the bar.

"Dawn!"

The high-pitched yell carried over the pounding drums from somewhere to her right. She turned and spotted Eric immediately, standing right behind a smiling Amy.

What the hell?

Changing course, Dawn jogged to her best friend. "I saw the police cars - are you okay? Where's Sam? Did he hurt you?"

"I'm okay," Amy said, pulling her into a quick embrace. "Better than okay, actually. Sam got arrested for attempted assault. Or I think that's what they called it. And your friend Eric here..." She took a minute to shoot an adoring look at Dawn's nemesis. "He's offered to stay on the couch until we're sure Sam's behind bars for good. Just to make sure the house is safe from Sam's minions. Isn't that sweet of him?"

The look in her eye irritated Dawn, and she couldn't even glance at Eric. "Um, that's nice of him, but probably not necessary. They're taking Sam into custody, right? This is the second time he's violated the restraining order. I can't imagine they'll let him out again."

"It's no trouble," Eric said, forcing her to look at him out of politeness. There was a challenge in his eyes, but he didn't know what he'd signed up for. Not yet. "You know I'm a sucker for a pretty face." He winked, and then smiled down at Amy when she grinned up at him.

"You get two for the price of one this time, big guy," she said, giggling when he raised his eyebrows. "Dawn and I are roommates, so you'll be protecting her too. It'll be fun!"

Eric's gaze met Dawn's over the top of Amy's head. Green flecked with hazel, she'd always been drawn to his eyes, but the intensity reflected back scared her. He was a predator, plain and simple, and while he seemed harmless, she sensed a reserve of energy within him used only on special occasions.

"Yeah, Dawn, it'll be fun," he mimicked, the mocking tone not lost on her as he turned his attention back to Amy. "Let me drive you home. I've got clean clothes in the truck, and you can show me how to work the remote."

"Deal," Amy said, clearly enamored as she grabbed his hand and started pulling him toward the door. "You'll catch up, right Dawn? In a while?" She gave Dawn a look she hadn't seen in awhile, the one that meant, "stay away until I'm done getting laid". Dawn barely managed to stifle an eye roll at the dramatics, though she couldn't quite tamp down the jealousy rearing its ugly head.

Waving her hands, she shooed them away. "Go ahead. I think I'll have a drink. Maybe two." She watched them walk out the door, Eric's arm protectively wrapped around Amy's waist. Running her hand through her hair, she turned to go to the bar, only to find Tweetle-red and Tweetle-redder standing right behind her, one of them holding out a shot, the other a beer bottle.

"We thought you could use this," the one with the shot said, offering it up. Dawn tossed it back, her opinion of the two rising by the second. When she was done, the other handed over the beer. "And this. Wanna come sit down?"

She looked at one, then the other. There was something about how they were looking at her...

Aw, crap.

Setting the bottle and glass down on a nearby table, she shook her head. "Sorry, ladies, but I need to get going. Thanks for the...um...drinks." Spinning on her heel she made a beeline for the door, vowing to purge her wardrobe of flannel very soon.

In the car with her key in the ignition, she paused, trying to decide where to go. After several indecisive minutes, she started the engine. Screw Amy's fun. Or not, if she had anything to say about it.

The Pile Driver

* * *

Eric considered rolling over and closing his eyes as he heard the front door open. He'd been surprised that Dawn and Amy were roommates, but pleasantly so. Unfortunately, she didn't seem to be too keen on him camping out on their couch for some reason. Still, he couldn't just let Amy go home alone, just in case her ex happened to make bail. He'd seen it happen before, and after years of protecting his mom from his dad, he wasn't walking away. Besides, maybe he could get under Dawn's prickly side and figure out what bothered her so much about him. Women didn't normally just brush him off, but she always kept him at arm's length. This was the perfect opportunity to catch her off guard and find out what she was really thinking.

He listened to her footsteps go past the living room to the kitchen. Maybe she wouldn't even see him - he'd left the light off on purpose, not wanting Amy to see it on and realize his excuse about being really tired after work was just that. A light glowed briefly in the hall, then went out. The house was quiet and he frowned, wondering where she'd gone. The only set of stairs to the bedrooms was near the front door - had she somehow snuck past him?

Or was it someone else in the house?

He rolled off the couch to the floor and got to his feet, moving silently in the dark thanks to a few years doing special ops in the army. Having memorized the layout of the room before he sent Amy to bed, he reached the doorway without making any noise and flattened himself against the wall. Someone was on the other side of the door. He could just barely hear shallow breathing then a small gasp as a board creaked under foot. He reached around the doorjamb, grabbed a handful of material and pulled the intruder into the room and onto a thick rug, pinning her down with his body.

Her.

Too late, he realized that the body under his was soft, small, and entirely too rounded to be male. The scent that hit his nose was alcohol mixed with earth and something flowery that only one person he knew ever smelled like.

"Dawn?"

"Yes, you oaf. Now get off of me. All that muscle weighs a ton."

She sounded annoyed, but there was something else in her voice that indicated she wasn't as inconvenienced as she wanted him to think. He pushed one leg, then the other between hers, and held himself up on his elbows, but didn't get up.

"Is that better? And thanks for noticing it's all muscle. Most women dig that."

An exasperated sigh escaped her lips. "I'm not most women. And I was just going to my room. Now are you going to let me up?"

Eric thought about it for a second as he gazed down at her in the dark. Her features were blurred and softer, but still readable. And her eyes were telling a different story than her mouth.

"What would you do if I kissed you?" he asked, stroking her hair off the side of her face.

She swallowed hard, the movement making her breasts rise against his chest. "You probably shouldn't."

He smiled at that, lowering himself so his lips were just centimeters from hers.

"I rarely do what I should."

Chapter Three

Eric's lips were warm, soft, and tasted of chocolate, making Dawn moan in appreciation as he kissed her. Embarrassed, she tried to push him away, but he only pulled his head back a little to grin at her in the darkness.

"Your hands say no, but your mouth says yes. Help me out here, Dawn. Which part of your delicious body do I listen to?"

Her first inclination was to curl her fingers into the tight t-shirt they were resting on and pull him down for another kiss. Still feeling a bit raw from everything that had happened at the bar, she ignored it.

"I guess that depends on which part of Amy's body you listened to earlier. Or those twins, though judging from the way they hit on me when you left, I doubt you would have gotten very far with them."

Eric laughed, the sound moving through the length of his body and vibrating into her own. Nestled between her legs as he was, she felt the length of his rigid cock pressing against her inner thigh and promising the ride of her life. Liquid heat seeped out from her core and she knew it would be all too easy for him to call her bluff, if he was so inclined.

"Someone's jealous," he gently mocked. "And here I thought you didn't care. Reason to celebrate, don't you think?" He kissed her again, shifting to position himself more perfectly at the apex of her thighs. It was all she could do not to raise her hips to meet his. Her traitorous hands slid up and over his shoulders to grasp the back of his neck. Soft, silky strands floated through her fingers as he nibbled on her lower lip. She barely held on to her thoughts as one of his hands found one of her breasts and teased the already hard nipple unmercifully until she was arching up against him to beg for more.

Earlier events no longer had any bearing as Dawn gave in to her primal side. She wanted this man, more than she'd wanted anything in a long time. Like her favorite dessert, she'd indulge just this once, and deal with the fallout later.

Wrapping her legs around his to invite him closer, she held on tight and kissed him back with all the pent up energy she'd been hiding whenever he was around. With a groan of approval, Eric ground his hips against her center and grinned against her lips.

"Good choice," he said, moving down to kiss the base of her throat. The intimate touch sent a shiver through her neck, and she wondered briefly if she'd be able to handle the intensity he promised. Then his mouth was latched onto her breast, and she tried to remember when he'd managed to unbutton her shirt and unhook her bra. Not that it mattered. He laved and suckled her hard nipple, his tongue decimating any last thought she might have as it flicked over the tender nub. A hand slipped between her thighs to rub over her throbbing clit, and it was all she could do not to cry out for more.

"You have too many clothes on," he whispered, his fingers working at the zipper of her jeans. "I want to see you naked, watch my cock sliding into your soaking pussy. You'd like that, wouldn't you Dawn? Do you want me to fuck you?"

"Yes," she breathed, pushing her pants and panties off her hips and kicking free. "Inside me. Now."

He leaned back just long enough to pull his shirt off and push his jeans down to his thighs. Dawn started to sit up and shrug out of her flannel, but he shook his head, placing a powerful hand in the center of her chest.

"Leave it," he said, lowering himself over her again. "There's no time."

Then the thick head of his cock was probing at her entrance, and she lifted her legs to wrap around his ass as he slid inside, seating himself fully in one long, slow motion.

In that moment, Dawn knew she'd made a horrible mistake.

* * *

Eric paused, letting Dawn adjust to him as he kissed her neck. She was tense under him, and he raised his head, studying her face as well as he could in the darkness. Was that moisture in her eyes?

"Hey," he said, swiping a thumb under one of her eyes. "Are you okay? Am I hurting you?" He started to pull out, but her feet locked him in place, her hands firm behind his neck.

"I...it's fine," she said, her voice softer than he'd ever heard it. "It's just...it's been a long time, is all.

66

Don't go, please." Capturing his hand with one of hers, she pressed a kiss into his palm, the tender gesture tugging at something deep within him. Something that told him this wasn't just a roll on the rug.

He laced his fingers through hers and pinned her hands over her head, then eased back and pushed inside her tight channel again. Slow, steady and deep, each thrust felt more like an affirmation of the bond that had always been between them in some form. As she arched up to meet him, mewling with hungry little sounds that drove him harder, faster, he knew that nothing between them was ever going to be the same again.

Fear and passion warred within as he responded to her urgent pleas. Pounding into her, he let instinct take over and ignored the part of his brain that told him this was all going to blow up in his face. Reaching down, he pressed his thumb against her clit and sent her spiraling over the edge, even as his own orgasm took him by surprise. Her inner muscles contracted around his cock, milking him so hard he almost couldn't take the intense sensations. When she finally released him, he slid out and rolled to the side, trying to pull her with him to lie in the crook of his arm.

She pulled away though, and he let her, still trying to catch his breath. When he finally realized she was on her feet, he sat up and caught her by the hand just as she would have turned away.

"Where are you going?" he asked, his voice raspy. "Are you sure you're okay?"

She nodded, her face unreadable from his vantage point in the dark. "I'm fine." She pulled her hand away, and he let his fingers trail down the side of her leg. "I'm just...I'll go up to bed now."

Eric frowned. Something was definitely wrong, and if he let her leave now it was just going to get worse.

"No, wait," he said, pushing up off the floor and taking her hand again and pulling her toward him. "Stay with me for awhile, please? I want to talk to you."

Her short, quiet laugh was bitter. "You never wanted to talk to me before - why would you want to now? Just because we fucked doesn't mean it has to mean anything, Eric. Thanks for the...uh...fun night. Sleep well."

He watched her go, his mind reeling as he tried to remember the last time they'd had a conversation.

Chapter Four

Dawn looked at the clock on the wall, and hurried to gather her things. She hadn't slept more than an hour the night before, and had left the house early to avoid seeing Eric. He'd been busy on the site all day, and if she was quick enough, she wouldn't have to talk to him tonight either.

They'd have to talk eventually, she knew. But every time she thought about it she was embarrassed by how much she'd revealed after that mind-blowing, once-in-a-lifetime encounter on the rug last night. As she tossed her purse over her shoulder, she rolled her eyes, knowing exactly what would happen when she finally faced him. He'd ask her out on a date - a pity date, because he'd either feel bad for her, or he'd want to sleep with her again. She'd have to say no, of

69

course, because no self-respecting woman would accept a pity date, right?

Then again, no self-respecting woman would have slept with a man she knew would break her heart.

She shook her head and turned off the lights. Last night she'd had a moment of weakness. One that had probably ruined her for good, because she was fairly certain that there weren't too many men who could live up to that performance. She'd do well to just file the whole thing under great life experiences, and move on.

She reached for the door just as it swung open, catching her in the shoulder and knocking her off balance. The lights came on, and Eric swore under his breath as he looked down at her, anger etched in the lines around his eyes.

"Good - you're still here. Are you okay? I didn't see you..." He knelt down beside her, concern mixing with frustration in his voice. He reached out to touch her, then pulled back. The uncertainty played on Dawn's sympathies like nothing else could.

"I'm fine," she said, moving her legs to prove it. "You...I thought you'd left." She hadn't, of course, but it seemed like the right thing to say. He sat back on his heels and studied her for a minute, that assessing gaze her undoing. Heaven help her, she'd fuck him again if he offered. Gladly. Right here on the office floor.

Or maybe the couch, considering the soreness in her tailbone.

He remained silent for a long moment, his chocolate eyes never leaving hers. He swallowed, and Dawn licked her lips, keenly aware of his distinct smell. Remembering how those arms had felt around her, that hard, well-defined chest under her hands. Long fingers wrapped around her ankle, sliding slowly, ever so slowly up the inside of her leg as he moved in.

"Do you want to get dinner?" he asked, his voice low and raspy, driving her mad.

"No."

He nodded, those fingers tracing a path up her inner thigh, his touch so soft she'd swear it was a feather.

"Wanna talk about last night?"

She shook her head, spreading her legs wide enough for him to see the moisture seeping through her panties.

"No."

"Wanna fuck?"

"Yes."

71

* * *

Thank god. Eric leaned forward, dragging his fingers lightly over Dawn's thigh to barely brush over the front of her silky panties. She shifted, restless under his touch. Closing the distance, he pressed his lips to hers - once, twice, tasting leisurely as his fingers worked under the seam between her legs. He stroked her pussy, her readiness evident, and finally he thrust two fingers inside her wet sheath as he entered her mouth with his tongue.

She whimpered, and he felt the sound all the way to his cock straining against his jeans. Then he pulled his mouth away, knowing he needed to slow down if either of them wanted more than just a quickie on the floor.

Again.

But Dawn had other plans, it seemed. When he would have pulled back, she reached for the hem of his shirt, working it off his head in record time. Then her fingers were at his waistband, and he returned the favor, reaching up under her skirt to snap the thin elastic that held her underwear in place. She whimpered again as she freed his cock, and Eric's head spun as she palmed it, squeezing from base to tip and back down again. Her other hand pushed against his chest and he lay back on the floor, closing his eyes as he felt her kneel between his legs.

A tentative swipe of her tongue over the tip of his already sensitive dick was sweet torture, and he wasn't sure he'd be able to handle much more. Pushing up on his elbows, he looked down just as her lips were sinking on him, taking him deep and he jerked up into her mouth, unable to stop the impulse. She moaned around him, her head bobbing up and down, drawing him in and letting him out with a rhythm that drove him wild. The vibrations in her throat combined with the warm wet heat were just too much. He jerked again, shooting cum down her throat, expecting her to recoil like most women did. But she merely took him deeper, swallowing everything he had to give and milking him with her lips until he was completely spent.

Collapsing back to the floor, he took a few seconds to breathe, then opened his eyes, looking for Dawn. She was already on her feet, looking down at him with a confused, ready-to-run expression. He grabbed one of her ankles, determined not to let her run again.

"You're not leaving." It wasn't a question, and the irritated look on her face told him she'd noticed.

Trying to wrench her ankle free with no luck, she tucked her hair behind her ear with one hand.

"Actually, I am. Now let go. I need to get home."

The pulse under his fingers was beating fast, and she avoided his gaze as he rolled to his side, still holding onto her ankle. Finally pushing to his knees, he transferred his hold from her leg to her wrist and stood up, losing his jeans in the process.

Dawn wasn't quite successful at hiding her grin as she watched, and he smiled at her as he toed off the tennis shoes he'd changed into after work and stepped out of his pants.

"Shouldn't you be getting dressed?" she asked, tugging at her wrist a little to check his resolve in holding out.

He shook his head, pulling her up against him and wrapping his free arm around her waist.

"Not unless you want to finish this in your bed," he said, earning a confused frown. "We have some unfinished business to attend to, don't you think?"

Chapter Five

Yes.

The word flitted through Dawn's mind immediately, though she didn't have the chance to say it as Eric bent to whisper soft little kisses gently against her lips. He'd finally released her wrist, but both of his arms were wrapped around her waist, and she knew she didn't have a chance against the sculptured biceps under her hands.

Or maybe she just didn't want to let go.

He moved backward, one deliberate step at a time as he kissed and lapped at her mouth. His teasing tongue politely requested entry and she gave it without hesitation, enjoying the gentle strokes and male taste of him until her knees hit something soft.

She tried to pull away so she could look, but only caught a glimpse of the sofa over her shoulders. Eric gave her the tiniest push and she found herself sitting in front of him. Looking up, she licked her lips and smiled.

"A snack? For me?"

Eric wagged a stern finger at her, grinning as he knelt down between her legs. "Uh-uh. It's my turn, honey, so you just lay back and get comfy."

Sticking her lower lip out in a pout, she giggled when he leaned over to kiss it away, pushing gently on her shoulders as he did. She lay back as he'd instructed, and stared at the ceiling. She appreciated the gesture, but in her very limited experience, men only went down on women out of obligation. She'd never met one who liked it, and certainly never one who could bring her to orgasm with his tongue and fingers. Resisting the urge to sigh, she consoled herself with the fact that it would probably be over very soon.

And then what?

His hands slipped between her thighs and urged them open wider. She obliged, waiting patiently for that first tentative touch. When it didn't come, she wondered if he'd changed his mind, and moved to sit up.

76

"Don't move," Eric said quietly. The words were more of a request than a command, and Dawn fell back to the couch, twitching when one calloused finger slid down the inside of her right leg. It traveled a particular path, winding and looping leisurely across her skin until it reached her inner ankle. When his lips closed over her big toe, she cried out at the unexpected sensation and her eyes closed as she arched her back, thrusting her breasts high in the air.

"Wow," he breathed, placing tiny kisses up the front of her left leg. "You're stunning."

She considered answering, but didn't have a clue what to say. 'Thank you" seemed so...inadequate. And then he was moving again, one hand reaching up push her shirt and bra out of the way to play with her nipple, the other spreading her wide as he finally reached her core. His fingers tweaked and tugged at her breast as he placed tiny kisses over the inside of her thighs, carefully avoiding the one place she wanted him most.

When he finally licked a long, slow swath over her core and sucked her clit into his mouth, she couldn't hold back any longer. Arching up and crying out, she came hard against his mouth. He groaned, lapping up every bit of her juices as his hands slowly caressed her legs.

When she finally was able to open her eyes, it was to see him standing over her with a satisfied look on his face. He held out a hand and she took it, allowing him to pull her to her feet. Her skirt fell down to cover her nakedness, and she straightened the rest of her clothing as well as she could, turning to find him dressed and waiting for her.

"I'm not sure what to say," she said, walking over to get her purse. "I...can't really believe we did that. Here." The heat rose in her cheeks as she looked around, thankful that the only video surveillance for the job was outside.

"Do we need to go check on Amy? Have you heard from her today?" He sounded normal, and for some reason that irritated Dawn.

She shook her head, moving past him toward the door. "She went to stay with that cop who's been helping her out for a few days. Apparently he offered, and she couldn't say no. So you're officially relieved of your watch dog duties." She chuckled nervously, holding the door open for him.

He reached out and took the handle, motioning for her to go first.

"Even better," he said, turning the handle to check the lock as he pulled the door shut behind him.

"We'll get take out, and then you're going to take me home with you. We need to talk."

* * *

Eric waited as Dawn fumbled with the key, the heat from their dinner welcome on his hands. She'd been quiet since they left the trailer, and while he didn't relish the thought of this conversation, he knew they had to do something if they were going to continue working together. Clearing the air seemed like a good idea. When she finally opened her front door, he followed her inside and kicked it shut with his heel, waiting as she locked it and put her keys and purse down.

"Where do you want to eat?" he asked, not surprised when she didn't meet his stare.

She pointed straight down the hall. "The kitchen's fine." She led the way, opening a cupboard when they entered the small room and taking out two plates to set on the table as he put the food down. Turning her back to him again, she collected silverware and two glasses before she returned.

Eric took the glasses out of her hand and set them on the table, waiting until she released the utensils before he took her hands and pulled her

79

close. Pressing a soft kiss against her lips, he pulled back and smiled down at her.

"I thought women liked to talk," he teased, keeping his tone light. "Here I am, trying to do the right thing, and you go all guy on me. What's on your mind, Dawn?"

She shrugged, moving out of his embrace as she reached for the glasses. "I'm sorry. It's been a long day, and I'm not sure what I'm feeling, or doing, or should be doing." She brought water back to the table and sat down, gesturing for him to sit as well before she reached for one of the take-out containers. "Honestly Eric, I think I made a colossal mistake sleeping with you, and I'm not really sure how or if I can fix it."

He thought about that for a minute, helping himself to the sweet and sour chicken. "Okay. That's a start. I guess I'd like to know why sleeping with me was a mistake. 'Cause it sure didn't feel like one to me." He wiggled his eyebrows and grinned at her disapproving look. "What? We had a good time, I thought. Twice."

"Yeah, but was that all it was? A good time?" She shook her head, her eyes focused on her food. "I thought I could be okay with that, but now I'm not sure I can. And that doesn't make any sense, because I hardly know you."

Eric nodded. "Fair enough. So what do you want then? Dinner? Movies? Walks in the moonlight? Because I'm not exactly that kind of guy. Well..." he surveyed the table pointedly, "I am a dinner kind of guy, apparently." He chuckled, pleased when her lips turned up just a little.

She put her fork down and finally looked at him, obviously confused and frustrated. "I want to get to know you. And I...I guess I want you to want to get to know me too."

He frowned. "Why wouldn't I want to get to know you?" Reaching across the table he took her hand, tracing her palm with his thumb. "I'll let you in on a little secret. I've been interested in getting to know you ever since we met. You just shut me down every time I tried to talk to you. Actually, you're one of the prickliest women I know, Dawn. Why is that?"

She put her fork down, heat creeping up into her face. "Prickly? Keeping a professional distance does not make me prickly. It makes me smart enough to stay out of relationships that will just cause trouble in the future." She took a sip of water, looking away from Eric's all too assessing eyes.

"You mean trouble like some idiot breaking your heart," he said, stating the fact rather than asking the question. She shrugged, picking up her fork again and toying with the food on her plate.

"Not just that. Dating people you work with can end up badly in other ways too. Sometimes people even lose their jobs. It's just not a good idea. Which is why I never should have..." she couldn't bring herself to say the words, but one glance at his face told her he already knew.

"You never should have slept with me because we work together. Sort of."

She nodded, slowly. "That, and I didn't want to be number eight this month. Or any month. Why do you always have a different girl on your arm, anyways? Is it boredom, or that tired 'afraid of commitment' thing? I don't know how you stand it, all those perfect women who all seem to share the same single brain cell. Although I guess you don't really talk to them though, do you? So I should feel special, I suppose."

Her snarky tone earned a raised eyebrow, and Eric crossed his arms over his chest, just staring at her with that questioning look. The one that told her she was playing with fire. She took a bite of food, even though she wasn't hungry and chewed slowly, staring down at her plate. Any minute now, he'd get up and walk away. It was inevitable, but she was determined not to say anything, not to cry when he left.

"It's actually simpler than that," he said finally, and she snapped her gaze up to meet his, unable to hide her surprise, which seemed to amuse him. "I like women. A lot. And I see no reason not to enjoy them at every opportunity, providing they're willing. Until now, at least."

She finished the last of her wine, her hand trembling a little as she set it down. Hopefully he didn't notice. "What makes me different?" She looked down at herself, and the baggy white sweater she'd pulled on over jeans. "Aside from not being anything like a supermodel, I mean."

He thought for a moment and then leaned forward, looking into her eyes. "Honestly Dawn? I don't know. But there's definitely something about you that is different from all those other girls, and I want to find out what it is. I'm sure you know I'm very attracted to you physically, but there's something more there. Don't you feel it? Or is it just me, feeling the connection between us? Do you believe in fate?"

She laughed, breaking eye contact and looking everywhere, anywhere else but at him. "Sorry, but no." She watched out of the corner of her eye as he leaned back in his chair and grinned.

"Me either," he said, pushing his chair back and rising to his feet. Dawn wondered, maybe even hoped that he would come around the table. To her. She was disappointed when he stayed where he was. "But I still think we should have dinner sometime. Like to-morrow night after work. I'll pick you up." Not wait-ing for an answer, he walked out the door.

Dawn watched him go, her eyes taking in that long, lean back and those tight buttocks she'd dug her nails into the night before. God, had it only been twenty-four hours? She surveyed the mess on the table, and started to organize it, then stopped to recap the situation.

Dinner. Tomorrow night. With a hot co-worker who would probably break her heart, get her fired and make her swear off men for another ten years. There's only one more question to answer, she thought as she gathered up a bottle of wine and a glass and headed for the bathtub.

"What the heck do I wear?"

Chapter Six

Eric pulled into Dawn's driveway, his cell phone ringing yet again. Turning the engine off, he checked the caller ID, and shook his head as her number popped up on the screen. Again. She hadn't shown up for work today, but had tried to call several times. He'd decided not to answer so she couldn't back out of their date. Now that he was here though...

"Hello?" He watched her figure stop pacing behind the curtain just before she replied.

"Oh good, you answered. Where have you been? I've been trying to call you all day." There was a frantic quality in her voice that he couldn't ignore, and he frowned, pushing the car door open.

"I'm sorry," he said, meaning it as he got out and headed to her door. "I'm here - what's wrong?"

She sighed, and he heard the regret in her tone. "I really wouldn't do this unless I had to, but something came up that I need to take care of tonight, and I didn't want you to think I was skipping out on you. Would it be okay if we rescheduled? Tomorrow, maybe?"

Eric leaned against the doorjamb, perplexed. He couldn't tell if she was lying or not, and she seemed sincere, but why wouldn't she tell him what she had to do?

"Sure, I guess. What's going on? Anything I can do to help?"

She laughed, but it wasn't a happy sound. "Thanks, but I should handle this myself. I appreciate the offer though, and thanks for not being mad about it. Tomorrow, okay?"

"Sure," he nodded, slowly backing away from the door. "Call me if you need me. Any thing, any time. Promise?" He watched her through the window, nodding her head as her answer came through the phone.

"Yes. Promise. Thanks for understanding."

The line went dead, and Eric considered knocking on the door, making her tell him what was going on. But the fact that he knew so little about her stopped him - maybe she had a good reason for whatever she was hiding. The urge to help was strong and it was a force of will to walk back to his car and get inside. He backed out of the driveway and drove home, his gut telling him he should have stayed, should have done what he could to help.

By ten that night, Eric couldn't stand it any longer. He dialed her number, and she picked up almost immediately.

"Eric? Is everything okay? It's pretty late..." She sounded tired and beat down, and he wished he could make whatever was going on stop for her.

He chuckled. "I think you just stole my line. I was calling to see how you were doing, after whatever happened today. So...how are you?"

"I'm...okay, I guess. Really tired. It's been a crazy day. But it's sweet of you to check up on me. I appreciate it." Her voice was shaky, and he could have sworn he heard a sniffle or two. Knowing the little that he knew about her, Dawn wouldn't ever ask for help though. And he was tired of sitting around doing nothing. It wasn't in his nature to let a woman in obvious distress stay that way.

"Are you at home?" he asked, reaching for his jacket and keys.

"Yes - I just got here a few minutes before you called. Why?"

He walked out the door and got in his car, turning the key in the ignition. "Stay put. I'm coming over."

87

* * *

"No...wait...Eric?" Dawn hung up the phone with a sigh when she realized he'd already disconnected. The last thing she felt like doing was entertaining people after a long and stressful day, but she supposed she owed him a few minutes at least. And an explanation. She hadn't wanted to burden him with her problems earlier, and she still didn't, but for some reason he seemed genuinely interested. Confiding in people wasn't her strong suit - it never had been, but maybe it was time that changed.

Too tired to change out of the sweats she'd put on just before Eric called, she closed her eyes and curled up on the couch to wait. When she opened her eyes again she was lying on her bed in the dark, and a warm, hard body was pressed against her back - presumably the owner of the large hand cupping her breast.

"Eric?" she whispered sleepily, recognizing his distinct scent and the feel of his touch. "What happened? How--"

"Shhh..." he released her breast, stroking her arm with the lightest touch and kissing the side of her neck. "You were fast asleep on the couch when I got here. The door was unlocked. I thought you'd be more comfortable in bed...and I'm not enough of a boy scout to sleep on the couch."

She nodded, her eyelids drifting down again even as she felt his cock pulsing against the crack of her ass. Men. "You said no sex before dinner," she mumbled, feeling his lips turn up in a smile against her shoulder. "Did you change your mind?"

"I don't think that's exactly what I said." He chuckled and kissed her shoulder, then her neck again. "Besides, we're not having sex. We're sleeping. Now rest."

"Yes sir," she whispered, fading back into the ether.

A sliver of light penetrated her bedroom curtains when she woke. Eric was kissing her neck again, trailing his fingers down the side of her ribs. She moved restlessly under his touch, snuggling closer as his cock throbbed hard against her backside again. Two fingers tugged at her nipple, sending delicious zings straight to her core. Her legs were restless, and the top one slid backward over his thick thigh, opening her for his pleasure. His fingers found her center, drawing lazy circles over her sensitive clit as she gyrated against his hand. She whimpered, thrusting her breasts out and using her own hands to massage the tender tips. Then he shifted, positioning his cock at her entrance and rubbing it over her pussy to coat it with her juices. She cried out and pressed against him, wanting, needing to feel him inside her again.

"Please Eric. Now," she begged, and he pressed inside slowly, inch by inch until he filled her completely. She sighed with relief, grasping him with her inner walls as he retreated.

"Damn," he breathed in her ear, suckling on her lobe as he began to thrust in and out, in and out. "This is not a mistake, Dawn. Don't ever think that. Promise me."

She nodded as his thumb found her clit and stroked in time to his cock. "I promise," she whispered, barely able to speak as the pressure built under his deliberate movements. She bucked against him, needing more. "Faster," she said, shifting for a better angle. "Oh yeah. Right there...oh god..."

His lips closed over her neck and the warm kiss shot through her body like an electrical current, taking her over the edge in a flash of pure white pleasure.

* * *

As she slowly came down from one of the best orgasms she'd ever had, Dawn was aware of Eric stroking her arm, his fingers moving languidly over her heated skin. Turning toward him, she couldn't help but return his smile.

"Good morning," he said, his raspy voice one of the sexiest things she'd ever heard. "Sleep well?"

She nodded. "Best in a long time. I'm glad you were here." She turned away, embarrassed at the admission and he chuckled, placing a quick kiss on her neck.

"Get dressed," he said, moving off the bed. She turned back to watch him pull on his jeans, leaving the button undone. "I'll make breakfast, and we can talk, okay?"

She looked at the clock and then opened her mouth to protest but he held up a hand.

"I already called and told them we wouldn't be in today. You could use a day off." One sly grin and he walked out, not giving her a chance to respond.

Dawn closed her eyes, imagining all the rumors that would undoubtedly be spreading about them. With a sigh, she rolled out of bed and headed for the bathroom. She'd have to talk to Eric about work and personal boundaries, but not until she had a shower and coffee.

Fifteen minutes later she followed the smell of sausage to the kitchen. Where had he found sausage?

The table was set for two, with syrup, a plate stacked with waffles, butter, the sausage and two cups of coffee. Standing at the stove, Eric looked over his shoulder at her when she came in.

"Right on time," he said, transferring an egg from the frying pan to a plate. Damn. Who knew a man could look so good standing at the stove? "Help yourself. One egg or two?"

"Um...one, I guess." Dawn sat in her normal chair, flabbergasted by the meal. "Where did you get all this food? I'm sure I didn't have most of this stuff on hand...and I don't own a waffle iron."

He shrugged, putting one egg on her plate before he sat down across from her. "I was going to make you breakfast last night, in case you hadn't eaten. So I brought it all with me, and when you were asleep, I figured it would be just as good in the morning." He took a sip of coffee. "Don't get too excited. The waffles are the made-from-frozen kind." He winked then started filling his plate.

"I don't really know what to say," Dawn said, pouring syrup over her waffles. Had a guy ever made her breakfast before? She didn't think so, but she could sure get used to it. "Thank you."

He nodded. "You're welcome. So, tell me what happened yesterday."

She thought for a moment, finishing the bite
she'd taken and following it with a sip of coffee.
"Amy called yesterday just as I was leaving for work.
Her ex - the one from the bar - broke into Sergeant
Branson's house early yesterday morning and tried to
kill her. The sergeant was shot, and Amy was beaten
up pretty badly, but I guess there were officers close
by who caught Sam and arrested him for attempted
murder and a bunch of other things."

"Wow," Eric said, leaning back in his chair to
listen. "Sounds crazy. Is she going to be okay? And is
the officer okay?"

Dawn shrugged. "Amy will heal, but the sergeant
is still in intensive care. It's touch and go, I guess, and
Amy's taking it pretty hard. I was at the hospital most
of the day yesterday, just sitting with her and trying to
make sure she was comfortable and had what she
needed. I was planning to go up again today after
work, and check on the sergeant while I'm at it."

Eric finished the last of his meal, then started
gathering up the dishes. "Let me clean up here, and
we'll go together. I can check on Sergeant Branson
while you sit with Amy. Is there anything you'd like to
take her? Some real food, maybe?"

"A few things," Dawn said, moisture welling in
her eyes. "Are you sure you want to spend your day at

the hospital like that? I mean, I can just call you when I get home or something...you really don't have to wait around for me."

He came around the table to stand beside her, looked down and cradled the side of her face with one hand. "I know how tough it is, seeing someone you love in the hospital after something like this. I want to help."

Chapter Eight

Eric looked down at Dawn, her beautiful eyes still a little sleepy as they narrowed with curiosity. Such a complex woman, but down deep, she had the same needs as anyone else. He should have pushed to get to know her a long time ago.

"How?" she asked, leaning into his touch as she tilted her head. "How do you know what it's like?"

Letting his fingers drop, he looked away, taking a breath and letting it out slowly before he could answer. "My dad wasn't a nice guy. He had a gambling problem, and losing made him mad. My mom ended up in the way more often than not, until I was old enough to step in. We spent some time at the hospital, she and I." He shrugged it off, not really caring to dwell on the past as he smiled down at Dawn again.

"We survived though, and the old man didn't, so it's all good."

She reached out to take his hand, squeezing it gently as she stood up. "I'm so sorry - that must have been really hard. Is your mom..."

"Still living? As a matter of fact, she is. I'll introduce you sometime. And maybe Amy too." He leaned down to press a kiss against her lips, loving the sweet taste of her mingled with orange juice and syrup. Not to mention the way her body pressed so naturally into his. "Are you ready to go?"

She nodded, rising up on tip-toe for one more kiss before she turned away. "Just let me get my shoes."

* * *

Ten hours later, he opened the door to his apartment and followed her inside. Locking the door, he turned and put both hands on her shoulders, using slow motions to massage away the stress that had taken over the moment they'd arrived at the hospital. It had been a veritable zoo with all the press from an officer shooting, and they'd had their hands full running interference for Amy. Everyone wanted to talk to her, it seemed, since the sergeant had been protecting her when he was shot. By the time they all left, most without a story, Amy had been completely worn out and Eric had taken Dawn out for a quick dinner, then invited her back to his place.

"I'll pay you a million bucks if you'll just keep doing that all night," Dawn moaned, leaning back into his touch. He chuckled, bending to place a kiss on her neck as he slid his hands down her arms, giving little squeezes along the way.

"You keep moaning like that, and I'll rub wherever you want, darlin'." He meant it too. Just as soon as he could get her out of those clothes.

She laughed, her shoulders visibly relaxing as she turned to put her hands on his chest. "Well you did buy me dinner. I guess that counts as a date." Her smile fading, she looked up at him, an earnest look in her eyes. "Thank you for coming with me today. I don't know what I would have done without your help."

He kissed her, wrapping his arms around her waist. "It was my pleasure. Although I'm pretty sure you would have done just fine without me, so thanks for letting me help. I know that probably wasn't normal for you."

She winced, shaking her head. "I guess not. But I appreciate it all the same." Her lips turned up, and her tongue darted out to wet them, the small motion making his cock twitch. "In fact, I'd really like to show you how much I appreciate it..."

Dawn reached for the button on Eric's jeans, sinking to her knees. Grinning up at him she slid the zipper down and his cock fell hard and ready into her waiting palm. She licked her lips then tasted the head, earning a low moan.

"You like that?" she asked, taking him into her mouth and sucking his cock all the way to the back of her throat then slowly releasing it as she looked up into his eyes.

He shook his head, one hand tangling in her hair. "God yes, babe. So much." He stroked her hair as she laved and sucked, and she let him guide her movements. Moisture soaked her panties as she hummed around him, her nipples pebbling as the lace of her bra moved against them. When he leaned down to pull her up, she whimpered in protest, earning a chuckle as he scooped her up in his arms. She hung on to his neck as his lips descended on hers, his unique taste warm and comforting as he carried her to his bedroom. He laid her down on a dark cotton comforter and she watched as he shucked his jeans and shirt.

Settling between her legs he framed her face with his hands, his eyes never leaving hers as he entered her. Filling her all the way, he stopped, kissing her softly on the forehead, then her lips.

"We belong together," he said, sliding his hips back a little, then forward, the motion slow and lazy. Every nerve ending between Dawn's legs cried out for more as she tried to process his words. "I know it's fast, but I think you feel it too." He took another long, slow stroke, his cock driving her mad with desire. She clenched her inner walls around him, tightened her ankles around his ass trying to spur him on. But he resisted, leaning back even more to run a finger between her breasts.

"So beautiful, and so smart. I'm not letting you get away, Dawn." Leaning down he pulled one nipple into his mouth, sucking hard and then nipping the tip before moving within her again. "Tell me I can move in next week," he whispered in her ear.

Dawn opened her eyes, moving her hips against his again and trying to make sense of his words. Had he just asked to move in with her? In the middle of sex? And she was supposed to be able to answer now?

"Eric," she panted, pulling him down for a kiss even as she ground her hips against his again. "You can't ask me to think now. Or talk. Later, okay? Just fuck me."

He began to move, a steady rhythm of thrust and retreat and the tension started building deep within her. His mouth was everywhere on her, kissing her chest, her collarbone, her neck, her earlobe. Closing her eyes, she lost herself to the amazing sensations he created. Higher and higher she climbed, whimpering with absolute pleasure as she felt the crest nearing.

Eric kissed her neck again, his mouth right beside her ear as he thrust once more and shattered her world, his low words reverberating through her body as she came hard underneath him.

"I'm in love with you, Dawn."

Chapter Nine

As she tried to catch her breath, Dawn tried to make sense of Eric's declaration. They'd only started getting to know each other a few days ago. It just wasn't possible...

Eric shifted to the side, and even with her eyes closed she could feel him gazing down at her. Warm fingers smoothed over her forehead, gently pushing the hair from the side of her face.

"I can hear your thoughts," he said, his tone light. "I should warn you that running won't do any good. I'm quick on my feet." His chuckle was contagious, and she couldn't stop her lips from turning up, even though she still refused to open her eyes. His lips pressed against hers for a moment, soft and un-demanding.

"Come on, Dawn. Open your eyes. Don't be a coward."

Frowning, she looked up to see an amused expression on his face. "I'm not a coward," she said, earning an acknowledging nod.

"Good." He trailed a finger down her chest, then back up to the base of her neck. "Let's talk about this, then."

"I thought it guys hated to talk after sex. Or about relationships. Are you sure you're a guy?" She screeched as he tickled her ribs, then snuggled her tightly in his arms, her back to his front.

"I'd say I've sufficiently proven my male status," he said in her ear, his hot breath against her neck driving her wild. "Nice try though."

She shrugged, closing her eyes and enjoying the feel of his skin against hers. Resigned to the fact that there was no escape, she gave in. "What do you want from me, Eric?" She didn't really want to know the answer. What if it was something she couldn't give?

He kissed the side of her neck. "Another date, for starters," he said, surprising her. She nodded.

"Done."

He pressed his lips against the back of her shoulder. "A weekend together, just the two of us."

"Okay." So far, so good. Maybe he really did understand. They'd take it slow, spend more time together and see how things worked out...

"A key to your house."

Damn.

She untangled herself from his arms and shimmied off the bed, reaching for his shirt to pull over her head before she faced him. "I'm sorry, Eric, but it's just too soon. I'm incredibly independent, and I can't just leave that behind for a few great days and awesome sex. I'm not saying I don't feel...what you're feeling, but can't we just give it some more time? What's the hurry?"

He shook his head, rolling off the bed to pull on his jeans. "It doesn't feel rushed to me," he said, getting a clean shirt out of the dresser. "I'm in love with you, and I want to be with you, every day, and every night. How can that possibly go wrong?"

Her heart pounded as she watched him dressed, the anger in his voice telling her where the conversation was headed. "You could leave," she said in a half-whisper, scared to admit it, but needing him to know. To understand.

He laughed, a mocking sound as he worked his feet into his tennis shoes. "I think you've got that backward, sweetheart. Looks to me like you're the

103

one leaving, since this is my apartment. Get dressed. I'll take you home."

* * *

Eric was silent as he drove Dawn to her house. She wasn't talking either, and he didn't blame her. When he'd snapped at her in his apartment, he'd immediately wished he could take it back. At the same time, he just didn't understand why she was still so insecure about their relationship. Her lack of faith raised questions he didn't really want to deal with just now, but they'd have to be addressed eventually. Or not, if Dawn decided to just walk away for good. It wouldn't surprise him after the way he'd acted.

He pulled into her driveway and she got out almost before the car stopped moving. He turned off the engine and followed her, knowing they couldn't just leave things this way.

"Dawn, wait," he said as she fumbled with the key to her front door. "I'm sorry, I am. I just - I want you to believe in us. In what we have together. Is that really so much to ask?"

She finally got the door open and stepped over the threshold, turning to block his path when Eric would have followed. "For me, yes, it is." She paused, looking at the ground for a moment before meeting his gaze. "I'm not going to move in with a guy I've been sleeping with for a few days, no matter how much chemistry we have. If you can't handle that, then don't call me again."

The door shut with a solid thunk, and Eric sighed. He went back to his car and backed onto the street, fighting the feeling that he wouldn't see her again. Unsure how he'd deal with that, or if he could, he went back to his place and slept fitfully, finally crawling out of bed around four in the morning for an ice cold shower.

* * *

"You did what?" Harry, the project builder raised his eyebrows over a cup of coffee at lunch. "I bet that didn't go over well."

Eric chuckled, shaking his head. "No it did not. And now she won't even talk to me." He'd been looking for Dawn when he came into the office trailer, but she was already gone when he got there. So he'd sat down to wait for her, dying to end the cold war between them. A few well-asked questions from Harry had brought the whole story out, though Eric wasn't sure what good it would do.

Harry sat back in his chair, folding his arms over his chest. "Son, that woman's been watching you switch partners for years now. You can't really expect her to just take your word for it that you're on the up and up...you need to give her time, prove that you're going to stick around. If you want my advice, you'll let her come to you, instead of trying to push things along so fast. What's the rush, anyway?"

Eric thought about that for a minute, then quickly gathered up his things.

"Where are you going, Son? Have you been listening to me?"

He nodded. "Every word, Harry. Thanks to you, I think I know what I need to do. I'll be back in a couple hours, okay?"

Chapter Ten

Dawn cautiously surveyed the parking lot after lunch, relieved that Eric's truck wasn't there. She was so confused, part of her wanting to just accept Eric's words and embrace the possibilities of a relationship with him. But it just felt too fast, like a big tidal wave sweeping her off her feet, and she needed to catch her breath before she drowned. Maybe in a couple days they could talk about it. If he was still interested, anyway.

She pushed the door open and went to her desk, stowing her purse in the normal drawer before she sat down. Finally looking at her desk, she shook her head slowly when she saw the blue velvet box. The thin, rectangular shape rejected the notion of a ring, though she didn't dare to examine that thought very long. She lifted the top to reveal a very shiny silver key nestled on the padded lining, and a folded piece of paper fell out onto the floor.

Setting the key down, she bent to retrieve the note, wondering if Eric was actually a stalker. Would he really have made a copy of her house key? And when? Heart racing in fear, she read the short message then read it again, blinking back tears.

Dawn,

I'm sorry I pushed you. I know you've been through a lot, and as someone recently pointed out, I'm not the poster-boy for commitment. I want to be with you though, and if that means giving you time and space, take as much as you need. This is a key to my apartment - my door is always open for you. Only you, with no strings attached. I'll be waiting.

Yours,

Eric

The door opened and she looked up, expecting him to be there. Instead, the project foreman clomped across the floor in his big work boots to re-fill his coffee cup, then left again, barely sparing her a nod on his way by. Oddly disappointed, she put the key and it's container into her purse and reluctantly went back to her work - or tried to. Twenty minutes later and still unable to concentrate, she left a message on Harry's desk that she wasn't feeling well, and went home to work things out in her head.

* * *

Eric's throat was tight and he rubbed his sweaty palms on his jeans before he went into the office. When he left the key on Dawn's desk, he'd been determined to stay away from her until she came to him, but as the day wore on he couldn't help himself. It would only be for a minute. Just to make sure she wasn't even more upset than she'd been last night. Then he'd leave her alone.

When she wasn't at her desk, fear nearly choked him. He checked the clock on the wall, but it was just barely past quitting time, and Dawn always stayed late. This couldn't be a good sign.

Harry came out of his office, casually propping a shoulder against the corner of the hall. "I don't know what you did, but she went home pretty quick after lunch. I hope you know what you're doing, son."

Eric shrugged. "Sure doesn't look like it. But the ball's in her court now. All I can do is wait."

"I often find that waiting just gives 'em more time to be angry," Harry said, his expression dubious. "Better to just have it out and get it over with, I say."

Eric nodded. "Me too, but I promised I'd give her space, and that's what I'll do, I guess. I'll see you tomorrow, Harry." He went to his truck and sat behind the wheel for a moment, contemplating stopping for dinner or going to the bar for a few drinks. If he went home, he'd just be alone. Waiting.

An hour later, he pulled into his parking spot, a bag of fast-food burgers and a six-pack of beer on the seat beside him. Beer in one hand, keys in the other and the bag nestled in the crook of his arm, he took the stairs one at a time, still dreading the silence he knew would greet him. Odd how just a few days spent in someone's company could make being alone less palatable.

At the end of the hall he turned the corner and looked down at his keys, then stopped as he saw the woman sitting on the floor with her back to his door. His pulse sped up, and he couldn't stop a grin from spreading over his lips.

"Dawn?"

His smile fell when she held up the key he'd given her. "I don't know what to say," he said, taking it from her. "I didn't mean--"

She got to her feet, looking at him with an oddly confident expression. "You could start with I'm sorry."

"I'm sorry." He searched her eyes, confused when he didn't find the anger he expected. "What am I sorry for this time, exactly?"

She moved closer, her mouth turning up slightly before she went up on tip-toes to give him a gentle kiss. "The key doesn't work," she whispered against his lips. "And if you didn't bring enough dinner to share..."

The bag hit the floor and he wrapped his arms around her waist, careful to keep the beer from smacking her on the butt. Capturing her mouth, he took his time kissing her soundly until she pushed against his chest.

"I'll get you a new key," he said, reluctantly releasing her as he picked up the bag and unlocked the door. "And if there's not enough here to share, you can have mine, as long as I can have you."

He put the food on the counter, hearing the deadbolt slide into place. When he turned around to make sure she was still there, he licked his lips and smiled. Somehow Dawn had stripped off her clothes in that short time, and she stood naked not three feet away, peering shyly up at him. He took two steps and dropped to his knees, his hands caressing her hips as his tongue found her clit. She whimpered a little, her fingers combing through his hair as she widened her stance to give him more room.

"Mmm..." she moaned, the sexy sound vibrating through his head. He looked up at her, waiting until she opened her eyes to look back before flicking her clit with his tongue.

She gasped and then chuckled when he did it again. "Would you like fries with that?"

###

About the Author

Trinity Marlow is the erotica pen name of Jamie DeBree. Born in Billings Montana, she resides there with her husband and two over-sized lap dogs. For a free serial draft of the next Naughty Encounters story, please visit TrinityMarlow.com or BrazenSnakeBooks.com.

Books by Trinity Marlow

Working Stiffs Collection

The Entertainer

The Pile Driver

Working Stiffs: Hardcore

The Mechanic

The Bouncer

The Paramedic

www.ingramcontent.com/pod-product-compliance
Lightning Source LLC
Chambersburg PA
CBHW021118130626
46554CB00002B/764